Aylmer Gowing

France Discrowned

and other poems

Aylmer Gowing

France Discrowned
and other poems

ISBN/EAN: 9783337267872

Printed in Europe, USA, Canada, Australia, Japan

Cover: Foto ©Andreas Hilbeck / pixelio.de

More available books at **www.hansebooks.com**

FRANCE DISCROWNED,

AND

OTHER POEMS.

BY EMILIA AYLMER BLAKE

Author of "Cæcilia Metella," "Leon de Beaumanoir,"
"A Life Race," &c.

LONDON:
CHAPMAN & HALL, 193, PICCADILLY.
1871.

Contents.

FRANCE DISCROWNED

'Ύβρις φυτεύει τύραννον.—SOPHOCLES.

"Nothing in his life
Became him like the leaving it; he died
As one that had been studied in his death,
To throw away the dearest thing he o wed,
As 'twere a careless trifle."—*Shakespeare*.

I.

Up rose the sun of Easter's holy morn,
   Rich in the joy of earth's reviving breath,
Who patient bore harsh winter's scath and scorn,
   Armed with immortal hope to conquer death ;
   Till once again her bosom, stirred beneath
The fire of youth, in all creation rife,
Woke to the freshness of remembered life.

II.

And life was strong within this breast of mine,
   The agony of life—the will to bear
Burthen and heat whose harvest is divine ;
   To win the promised crown of those who dare
   Wrestle with Fate and overcome Despair :
So nature worked in every living thing,
And wrung me with keen anguish of sweet spring.

III.

Then asked I, " Is the soul's desire in vain
 Unto the stars, which tells her, sorrow-bow'd,
Of love and glory ?"   And my heart with pain
 Grew hot within me, that I cried aloud :
 " Is there no help ? no rift amid the cloud ?
' Light, light, more light,' the poet's dying word,
Was't not the murmured moan of hope deferred ?"

IV.

" Light be, and light was," so the heavens and earth
 Were quickened in the womb of lasting night,
And sprung from nothing, perfect in their birth,
 Father of Spirits, to Thee ! Do Thou make light
 Where darkness is, bring down to mortal sight
Some pale reflex of Thy far heaven's sheen,
Lest our faith fail for what our eyes have seen !

V.

Ah me, fair France ! what seas of fire and blood
 Have swept thee from the haven of thy pride !
The sudden earthquake and the answering flood
 Have met thee with perdition on their tide,
 A mountain-heap of waters ! far and wide
They fling thee helpless on an iron shore,
Lost 'mid the shriek of winds and ocean's roar.

VI.

I stood as in a dream, and gazed—great ruth
  And sorrow fell upon me, as on one
The pleasure of whose eyes in early youth
  Is ta'en away, and hid from 'neath the sun,
  Returned to dust—who bears a life foredone,
Through the long, weary waste of widowed years,
Made rich for heaven with drops of earthly tears.

VII.

How art thou changed, thou Babylon of the West,
  Proud queen, whose smile was peace, whose frown
    made war
To shake the nations and their princes !   Rest
  Has come to thee unwilling, and a bar
  Is set to thy ambition's swell—So far
No farther !   Who hath ta'en away thy crown,
And sold thee to thy foes to tread thee down ?

VIII.

Where is the cause ?   Go, seek not far away,
  But in thy proper breast, the inborn curse :
The idol worship of thy god of clay,
  Bent to destroy and make of evil worse
  Through false desire of good, perdition's nurse ;
Thy prophet-king, who speaks, and thou art won ;
Whose name is Glory or Napoleon !

IX.

This is the cause, this only makes of thee
    A wonder and a pity unto men
Throughout the world—that such calamity
    Should come upon such greatness—yet again
    Shalt thou cast off the slough of shame, and then
Stronger and purer shalt arise, to prove
The chastening arm has stricken thee in love.

X.

In love, for thou wert faithless : power and grace
    Past measure were thy heritage, and thou
Couldst see no God above thy lofty place
    To worship and believe in—bend thy brow
    Beneath his hand laid heavy on thee now,
And live to bear again thy light on high,
The brightest beam of hope beneath the sky.

XI.

Fierce was the frenzy of untamèd hate
    That bound thee to a man to do his will :
Better it seemed to make his word thy fate
    Than suffer each variety of ill
    Inward contention works to heal or kill :
Rememberest thou that dark December day
Thy laws, thy honour passed beneath his sway ?

XII.

Was it a crime ?   Can evil bring forth good,
   Or dull the sharpness of calamity ?
Lo, search not then to find the stain of blood
   Upon the purple robes of Majesty :
   Napoleon shall fulfil his destiny,
More than a king—or less than basest slave,
Be thrust from forth the land he dared not save !

XIII.

Talk not of oaths, religion, duty, trust,
   The bonds of common men !   Another faith
Is found for him who reigns ; for reign he must
   Whose palace gates no pale remorse betrayeth
   To savage justice ; sacred from all scath,
Hath he not set to bar the surging hell—
Murder and Fear, and they shall serve him well !

XIV.

Was it a crime ?   Then shall he be assoiled
   Who gluts the multitude with bread and fame ;
Brisk Commerce now, and industry unspoiled
   Speed blithely 'neath the Ægis of a name,
   Filling the land with gold to cancel shame :
France thrives apace, and lo, a cry from far
Stirs in her breast the old fierce lust of war !

XV.

To arms ! the shadow of the Tricolor
   Stoops to the fury of the northern hail :
Help to the Turk !   Sinope's firelit shore
   Has seen a deed to make the heavens grow pale ;
   Ho ! speed the steamship ! spread the impatient sail,
To battle for the children of the sun :
O ! Monarch of the Franks—'tis wisely done !

XVI.

Hast not, by counsel, made thy quarrel just—
   Set Rome upon thy side ? whose changeless doom
Bade gather up from antiquated dust
   The key of entrance to Messiah's tomb :
   No more the infidel's disdain shall loom
O'er Christian rites—the Church's Eldest Son
Has spoke for Europe, and the pass is won.

XVII.

France shall be guardian of the holy places
   Too long defiled by Islam and the Turk :
France for the title of the Latin races !
   But lo, the Greek sets hand unto the work
   To make confusion !   'Ware the fires that lurk
'Neath pious seeming ; and the Moslem tell,
"Truly these Christians hate each other well !"

XVIII.

Hath Russia not a Father and a King
   No less than France and Rome?—a million hands
All armed, in simple trust unquestioning,
   To slay or to be slain for his commands?
"Ours the true faith above all other lands,"
Their cry. Remember we the mournful Word,
"Not peace I come to bring you, but a sword."

XIX.

Not peace when, in the name of injured Heaven,
   Man sits in judgment on his brother men,
Arms him with thunder and the blasting levin,
   To war 'gainst thoughts and consciences—yea, when
   His eye presumes to search beyond its ken
The hidden thing of God: woe worth that hour
Of evil passion clothed in lawless power!

XX.

The earth-born serf and his Imperial Lord
   Burn with one purpose—for Jerusalem
Be Stamboul surety, death the swift reward
   Of double-hearted Osmanli; on them
   The fiery flood no living hand can stem
Bursts forth—until a loud and bitter cry
From the dark Euxine wings their agony.

XXI.

To fill the utmost corners of the earth,
   To smite against the portals of the skies
To kindle vengeance on the household hearth,
   Indignant pity's flash in gentlest eyes:
   Shall not the Chivalry of Europe rise
To help the helpless, to redress foul wrong,
In battle 'gainst the oppression of the strong?

XXII.

Ours is the Cause, in England!   Side by side
   With France, too long our foe, we will put forth
Our flower of strength, in holy bonds allied,
   For death-grips with the Giant of the North,
Rather than bide in fear of him!   What worth
Is life without the ornament of life?
Up, men of Albion, gird ye to the strife!

XXIII.

And England at the call—a Spartan mother—
   Sends forth her sons to conquer or to die—
Her noblest with her least; and yet another
   With heart and voice makes answer to that cry—
   The voice of young, aspiring Italy—
Against oppression's might, by deed and word
Protesting with a hope which shall be heard.

XXIV.

And thou, divided Austria !—loth to fight
   Thy brother and thy friend, yet put to proof
By strong persuasion to defend the right,
   Merely by moral weight—dost hold aloof
   From all offence, as, for thine own behoof
No soldier in this war, but bear'st a hand
To drive the Imperial quarry to a stand.

XXV.

Be the end good, how shows the means in thee
   To spurn for that thy bond of gratitude
Sealed to the tamer of thy enemy,
   Who dwells within thy house at deadly feud,
   The fierce Hungarian, baffled, not subdued ?
Bitterly stings forgotten kindness—'ware
The locked embrace, the vengeance of the Bear !

XXVI.

O fool, that canst not ponder in thy heart
   The example of the wisest in their day !
Lo ! how the sable eagle broods apart,
   Biding the hour and the predestined prey,
   When all thy sand-bound fences shall give way :
Alike of Bonaparte and Royal Guelph
The creed is, " Heaven for all, each one for self."

B

XXVII.

Now are ye tunèd to the self-same note,
  One cry for War, the first-born son of hell:
Lo, on the lurid heaven your banners float;
  Napoleon's name of power hath bound the spell,
  The fury of the nations he shall quell
To bear him through the storm-blast;—whither lead
The desperate rider and the wingèd steed?

XXVIII.

What if your chief be other than ye deem,
  People and kings, upholders of his claim?
No human War-God—wondrous skilled to seem
  Sprung from the immortal race—yet not the same;
  To batten on an heritage of fame,
O how unlike his semblance! Full of guile,
'Neath the cold mockery of his joyless smile.

XXIX.

Why halt ye on the threshold of the scene,
  While your grim farce of " Help the Turk ?" breaks
    down
'Neath the world's laugh and hissing? Shiftless, mean
  Your policy, waiting while the Cause is won,
  And sore bested, Silistria holds her own
Intact and virgin still, by Allah's aid :
Dead 'neath her walls ten myriad Russ are laid!

XXX.

Not without cost of dearer lives, nor then
   Such fame, without good help of British hands
Was won to Islam—few devoted men,
   Stung by the shame upon our laggart bands,
   Curtius-like, sought a grave in Ister's sands ;
And many a song of Eastern bards shall tell
How Erin's son,[1] stout-hearted, fought and fell !

XXXI.

Blest they who died the hero's death ! for them
   Life's crowning glory was its bright release :
Oh, peers of England ! why will ye condemn
   Her manhood's flower of strength to waste in peace ?
   To rot in cold inaction, till surcease
From pain be borne upon the poison-breath
Of Allahdeen, and Devno's valley of death.

XXXII.

What make ye with our armies ? given with pride
   For duty's godlike tasks —oh, not for this !
To yield their lives in vain, where seas divide
   The eyelids closed to earth from Love's last kiss,
   Memory and herald of immortal bliss !
Fond arms shall clasp no more our heart's desire,
Consumed like grass on fever's bed of fire !

XXXIII.

Forward! the word is given at last; lie still
  Ye who have sunk to sleep—if life yet beat
Within your breast, arise! the bugles shrill,
  The summons has gone forth through camp and fleet;
  Not sightless death but mortal foes we meet:
No let, no pause, the struggle once begun,
For France or England, until all is won!

XXXIV.

Yet whither bound? Make answer to that word,
  Ye many-sounding trumpet-notes of Fame:
Show forth, hope's beacon-light, too long deferred
  Where best to crush the haughty Russian's claim,
  And crown our brows with glory, his with shame:
Our course lies for the far Crimean shore,
Such is Napoleon's will—we ask no more.

XXXV.

They rush, they swarm upon the lofty ships,
  A press of valiant men, with hearts that burn,
With shouts of victory upon their lips,
  That victory their blood hath yet to earn.
  Oh me! how many never shall return!
Like locust-flights they fill the hostile strand,
Or ocean waves borne in upon the land.

XXXVI.

Forward ! the Russian hordes have turned to bay ;
  They stand to bide our brunt by Alma's stream,
A name to be remembered from this day !
  Forward !—beneath the serried bayonets' gleam
  Each life suspended moves as in a dream :
The heavens grow black with smoke of iron showers,
Flies the word " Charge !" and Alma's heights are ours.

XXXVII.

Then was the hour for England and for France
  To whelm beneath the flood of victory
Sebastopol unarmed for their advance,
  And dumb with fear—had they but known !—oh why
  Did such a time and tide pass vainly by ?
Why must they stay to hear offended Fate
Ring in their ears the bitter scoff—" too late."

XXXVIII.

Unready, still unready ! slow delay
  Yields golden moments to the rallying foe ;
Or ere the weary conquerors plough their way
  Toward the grim fortress, now prepared, as though
  A nation's life-blood to the heart should flow :
There Prince and people gather up their strength ;
Dear must it cost us to prevail at length !

XXXIX.

Forth to his task, the griesly harvest-lord
   Fares with a laugh upon his visage dim ;
Swift plies the sickle 'neath his arm abhorred,
   Till many a lofty head and martial limb
   Cut down to earth, yields preciously to him :
Dark angel, bind and gather in much spoil,
Sheaves of brave lives the wages of thy toil !

XL.

O Death, we hail thee with high festival
   And sacrifice ! as erst the Argive maid [2]
Enriched destruction with the blood of all
   Whom tides and tempests to this coast betrayed,
   The ocean wanderer's sepulchre, and made
The Powers of darkness glad with rites like these,
Stern priestess of the Taurian Chersonese.

XLI.

How many a gallant spirit sought the doom
   Foreknown of Balaklava's fatal ride ;
Or found a grave unnoted in the gloom
   Of night and battle, by Tchernaya's tide ?
   When crushed battalions yielded not, but died
'Neath desperate odds, whose blood like water ran,
Upon the empurpled heights of Inkerman.

XLII.

The strife of Titans! man to man, as there
   Fate hung upon each single arm, they fight;
Till help to turn the scale of war they bear
   Came with the fire of France, and noonday light
   Was shed upon the world's most hideous sight—
Heaps of our fallen, pierced by Russian steel
When sinking life retained but strength to feel.

XLIII.

Scarce with the wreck of many a goodly form
   The greed of all-devouring Earth was fed,
When, frenzied by the demon of the storm,
   The Sea grew jealous, and a-hungerèd
   Rose up to claim her portion in the dead;
And shattered ships and corses strew the shore,
Whose stones, unsated, still cry out—" more, more !"

XLIV.

Then came sharp anguish of a bitter cold,
   To pierce the marrow with a burning frost,
That keen Crimean Winter's flaws enfold
   On barren hills a fever-stricken host,
   With strength diminishing when needed most;
Unclothed, unhousèd, grievously bestèd ;
The cruel sea scarce doles their daily bread.

XLV.

Ill fares precarious life that builds its trust
   On those wild waters—in their summer smile
Too like false woman ! Yet from these they must
   Take the bare wants of craving nature, while
   The pride of manhood stoops to uses vile,
Till living wretches envy those who die,
So best, to make an end of misery !

XLVI.

Death takes his own, and, making choice through all,
   Sweeps down the Moslems; thick as summer flies,
Condemned to rot in idleness, they fall,
   Or leaves in Autumn, they whose heart and eyes
   Seek battle as the gate of Paradise,
And hot with passionate lust of death, to toy
With the dark phantom, taste a bridegroom's joy.

XLVII.

Woe worth the treacherous counsel of a friend,
   That bade them traverse sea and land to foil
The foe that pressed their borders ! this their end,
   To feed corruption on an alien soil ;
   Day after day, with lamentable toil,
In shallow earth the dying lay the dead,
Scarce hid from sight—unseemly burièd.

XLVIII.

So that when lovely Spring put forth again
  On the dark ground her broidery of flowers,
And song and game and cheery laugh of men
  Could cheat the sorrow of the heavy hours ;
  The tempest clouds borne down in hail and showers
Lay bare those festering heaps to hateful light,
And on the living shed Infection's blight.

XLIX.

Then these, bound down to perish inch by inch,
  Food for the sightless Pestilence, without
A thought of yielding, in their desperate pinch
  Untaught to palter with despair or doubt,
  All that were left to suffer now, cry out
To sound the murderous assault—best so
To war with flesh and blood, to grasp their foe !

L.

Shall we then never make our stand inside
  These walls and baffling earthworks ? Shall we be
As those our comrades were, who tamely died
  While Turks, unaided, set Silistria free ?
  The booming of their cannon ceased, and we
Thought the doomed stronghold fallen, not relieved
Without our help—wherefore were we deceived ?

LI.

" Oh for the days when Britons stood alone
 Against the world in arms! our 'minished band
No longer 'mongst the French may hold our own,
 The post of peril on the hot right hand!
 Yet with divided counsels and command,
Lead on! once more these Cossack hordes shall hear
The ringing fury of the Northern cheer!"

LII.

Not since immortal spirits warred in heaven
 Have souls with such indomitable will
Met in the keen embrace of hate, and striven
 To give and bear the extremity of ill,
 Resisting unto blood, unmastered still;
Gods tread the earth in battle, like with like;
The skies bring forth the thunder as they strike.

LIII.

A nation's heart has risen behind those stones,
 To guard their envied jewel from surprise:
A nobler faith for days of shame atones,
 When fortune set before the Invader's eyes
 The holy city—had he snatched the prize—
Armed, and resisting now his fierce endeavour,
Foot by foot—life for life, bruised—bending, never!

LIV.

When in that hour, of God **and man** forsaken,
 Her people **lay,** expectant of the blow,
Yet turned **to meet** it with resolve unshaken,
 Women, ay, little children, **toiled** to show
 Such front of opposition to **the foe,**
As, by dear grace of heaven, might **render vain**
The occasion lost, that cometh **not again.**

LV.

Each one as for his own immortal soul,
 Ceaseless they worked, and put **their** trust in **God:**
Till they beheld upon each bristling knoll
 The slow approaches peer from 'neath the sod :
 " A miracle !" they **cry** ; "God's wrath hath trod
Upon the neck **of** pride—constrained by prayer,
His angel scatters horror and despair.

LVI.

" Among our enemies !"—ay, even so !
 He that should lead **the** Gaul to victory,[5]
Heeds not, beneath the hand of death laid low,
 The glory of the world, and lets pass by
 Time, priceless treasure of Eternity :
Palsied the arm to strike, there lives a hope
" **Russian** defence" with slower siege may cope.

LVII.

"Though myriad's die, live Russia and the Czar!"
   Their ramparts are the bosom of the brave;
Their fleet imprisoned stems the flood of war,
   Seven sunken ships defend beneath the wave
   The harbour-mouth close fastened as the grave:
So with their wealth and lives the valiant cherish
A nation's life—whose glory shall not perish!

LVIII.

Remember Moscow! Time hath worn away
   The cruel winter's cold, and summer shines
On earth in beauty, and a proud array
   Of valiant men refill the vacant lines,
   Whose doom the grass beneath their feet foresigns;
Of those who came last autumn, oh, how few
This second year the weary strife renew!

LIX.

"Zouaves advance the foremost!"   They attack,
   Break through the outworks of the Mamelon,
Rush in and slaughter, like a raging pack,
   By huntsman's horn and whip set madly on;
   Such their fierce hold upon the vantage won;
While burns the midnight welkin, cleft asunder
By storms of earth and Heaven's commingling thunder.

LX.

This stand-point safe, with hot, ungoverned haste,
　　Like pent-up steam their leader's fury burns ;
Inconstant France by sleight-of-hand would taste
　　Those fruits of Fame enduring patience earns ;
　　And England's chief o'erborne, reluctant learns
To yield the helm of Fate to Pelissier,
Untaught to heed when question meets his " yea."

LXI.

" To take from France the curse of Waterloo,
　　Her triumph now shall mark the self-same day;"
From noble Raglan in his anguish flew
　　The lightning message home t' entreat delay—
　　Swift answer bade him choose not, but obey :
Then be the assault—it cannot come too soon !
The ne'er forgotten eighteenth day of June.

LXII.

France flings her legions on the Malakoff,
　　Sole key of conquest, aim of all desire ;
This seized, Sebastopol is ours !—forced off
　　By arms of desperate men, by steel and fire,
　　Seven times the hosts of Gaul advance, retire,
Break in confusion, sink and die beneath
The giant stronghold, armèd to the teeth.

LXIII.

Through the grey dawn their signal-rocket ran,
   To tell the breach was gained, and bid advance
The English to the storm of the Redan :
   The Russ, unbroken 'neath the blows of France,
   Cast back the comrades of her evil chance ;
His ships and batteries give forth shot, mitrail,
That none can live beneath their deadly hail.

LXIV.

Perish that memory from out the world !
   Tell it not where our heroes' bones repose !
Men of our blood and warrior lineage, hurled
   From parapet to ditch, before their foes
   Were made a spectacle—on the strife uprose
The sun of Waterloo ; his noontide flame,
That day of glory, blushed upon our shame !

LXV.

Ours then to wait upon the Muscovite
   For mournful truce and burial of the slain ;
Through weary hours, to sicken o'er the sight
   Of wounded wretches, in their thirst and pain
   Beseeching aid of us—too long in vain !
Then brave men's eyes wept fire o'er many a head
Brought down in silence to the narrow bed.

LXVI.

Came sorrow unto all, to one, despair :[4]
 Sick with the loss and foul reproach, our chief
Sunk down beneath the load—too hard to bear—
 England had laid upon him : no relief
 For him beneath the sun ! the mortal grief
That silent bled within the true heart's core,
Found language in the living face no more !

LXVII.

So fate atones for fate—the Imperial form [5]
 In whose vast mould a nation's pulses beat,
Had given its beauty to enrich the worm :
 Sole lord of Russia's millions, it was meet
 His spirit, rather than endure defeat
Should taste of death ; nor unavengèd may
Such breath conclude itself in coffined clay.

LXVIII.

Nathless, no pause is given to human wrath :
 Light-hearted France, with will now firmly set
Unswerving, bends her to the bloody path
 Must yield her foot some coign of passage yet !
 Taught wisdom of the ant, her legions let
The sword have rest, while patient se'ennights twelve,
Ceaseless, the hot beleagurers pierce and delve.

LXIX.

Through sap and mine in endless labyrinth
   Like gnomes, the toilers of the earth, **they swarm,**
Strong in their multitudes; endurance winneth
   Their battle in the dark, till safe from harm
   The bold endeavour of an outstretched **arm**
Almost might lay the adventurous fingers' touch
On ramparts crumbling 'neath a conqueror's clutch.

LXX.

Shall Englishmen do likewise ? oh the mock
   Of effort, nature's stern denials foil !
Shall horsemen run a race upon the rock,
   Or oxen plough the niggard stony soil ?
   Loud preparation raised a mighty coil
To bring again disaster, with the crash
Of living men, whom desperate chieftains dash

LXXI.

Wide of the mark, upon the frustrate aim
   Fortune still shuns, though folly will attempt :
Again the slaughtered English heaped that same
   Fell ditch of the Redan—their death exempt,
   Through valour only, from their foe's contempt ;
Unworthy doom of heroes, to make good
The counsels of distraction with their blood !

LXXII.

The burden of that bitter day was theirs,[6]
   While the proud eagle of the Tricolour
Crowned the defence of Malakoff, unwares
   Changed to a citadel of France, before
   The swelling wave of victory broke, that bore
Frenchmen as lords within the ill-guarded prize
Snatched from the mid-day sleep of war-worn eyes.

LXXIII.

True to their standard, and the old renown
   Sprung with the fleur-de-lis, from noon till night
They held the lists 'gainst death—the sun went down
   Upon the fury of the doubtful fight—
   Then Britons thirsted for the morning light,
And fierce renewal of the battle, fain
To heal with life's last drops their honour's stain.

LXXIV.

Ay, little had that night to do with sleep!
   Shock upon shock foreshows the crack of doom,
While fiery columns from their craters leap
   To rend aloud the curtain of the gloom;
   In burning seas on high they spread, they loom;
The earth doth shake beneath them—stout hearts quail,
The stars amidst the trembling heavens grow pale.

D

LXXV.

Time bore another day—that Sabbath morn
　　Showed the fair city's queenly coronal
Of forts and fencèd batteries rent and torn
　　Like beggars' garments; ships that wont to gall
　　And rack with fire, her land-locked armament, all
Sunk in her port, for ever there to keep
Silent beneath the waters of the deep.

LXXVI.

Whither has vanished now the conqueror's dream,
　　White walls and golden domes?　Lo, desperate
Of help or remedy, in her last extreme
　　The Empress of the Euxine scorned to wait
　　Shame by a victor's fury consummate;
Met him, as Carthage met the Roman—bent
To 'scape by fire abhorrèd ravishment!

LXXVII.

'Tis done—the work of Titans! mountain heaps,
　　Iron and stone fire-mingled, bar pursuit;
While o'er the bridge across the harbour creeps,
　　In long, grey serpent-trail, a force of foot,
　　Sole salvage from the huge combustion.　Mute
The conqueror saw and hindered not, heart-wrung
By thoughts that found no shape upon the tongue.

LXXVIII.

This then the profit for such bitter cost
    The reckoning day of victory can tell;
The august dominion is not won, though lost,
    Whose guileful champions 'neath the fire of hell
    Rained down upon their roofs, till none could dwell
'Midst that hot siege and live, knew when to yield
Barren possession of the slaughter-field,

LXXIX.

And hurl defiance from their forts beyond
    The gulf, full-fed by unexhausted seas,
And blocked with wreck impervious, till the bond
    Of vengeance melt in vanity—are these
    The Allied powers would shape the world's decrees?
No more! the heavens alone their thunders roll
O'er the charred waste that was Sebastopol.

LXXX.

Enough! The Imperial arbiter of France
    Sickens of blood, the balm of wounded pride,
Content to close upon the happy chance
    That yields her rest with honour satisfied,
    And rich reward of glory, to abide
An heirloom of his sceptre, with increase
    Of power established by triumphant peace.

LXXXI.

Far be from him to press the bitter end
   Against a foe, beyond his proper need;
To share his part in honour with the friend
   Whose service earned for him the conqueror's meed;
   Now shall the Muscovite make act and deed
Of amity with him—if England will,
Or will she not—so holds his purpose still.

LXXXII.

And England hath surrendered at his pleasure,
   The ground beneath her feet, so hardly wrought
Out of that hostile soil, at cost past measure
   By tale of mortal compt; possession fraught
   With memories of her heroes slain, who fought
Duty's good fight and died; their bones lie cold
In foreign earth, as gems encased in gold.

LXXXIII.

Commit we to our foes with tender trust
   And graven prayer on stone, their place of rest
Made holy ground by that beloved dust
   Of English mould—our brightest and our best—
   While 'midst our desolate homesteads, unredressed,
The widow's wail is heard, and mothers weep
Their darlings locked in everlasting sleep.

LXXXIV.

And those yet nearer, in sweet hope betrothed
  To their first love, now faithful to the dead,
Hold weary life a thing accursèd, loathed,
  Reft of its joy, their heart is burièd
  Beside the slain, in that dim bridal bed
Where heroes wrapped in glory's crimson shrouds
Await the trumpet call from 'bove the clouds.

LXXXV.

With tears in sharper anguish shed than blood,
  Like Jeptha's living sacrifice, they moan
The bloom ungathered of their virginhood :
  Warm, radiant beauty, withering alone,
  Yearns for the lost, in dreams once more her own,
With passionate love that cannot pass away
From perished forms enwombed in clods of clay.

LXXXVI.

Shut from the earthly paradise of youth,
  Their light cut off by darkness, crushed in pain
Their souls' immortal longings—this is truth
  'Neath the veiled sun—this—all things else are **vain**
  Shadows men spend unquiet days to gain,
Possess, and know no joy ; our Father gives
Love's blessing to this world, by which it lives.

LXXXVII.

And now, though set on blood, Napoleon's throne
    Stands strong before the world in happiness :
Peace signed in Paris—thus a friend is won
    In Russia, England still his friend no less ;
    While all men praise him, Heaven is gained to bless
The importunate pleadings of unwearied prayer :
A son is born to him, his Empire's heir.

LXXXVIII.

So his long trouble sleeps secure beside
    The flower of earth-born beauty—loveliest
From Spain and Albion's blended stems, his bride—
    The burthen of his spirit, care-oppressed,
    Sunk on the snow-white roses of her breast ;
Fair Rhodope who charmed a monarch, fain
To quit the royal Austrian's cold disdain.[7]

LXXXIX.

Ay, Cæsar scorned can choose the better part
    In life's inheritance, heaven's gift of love ;
Some kindness nestles in that stony heart
    The gentle spell of beauty's touch can move ;
    Those cold, hard eyes a human passion prove,
And melt in tenderness and weeping joy
O'er the saved mother and her living boy.

XC.

Uneath within Ambition's fane may dwell
   The light divine of Nature's common ties ;
Yea, set upon the highest pinnacle
   Man's foot can touch, the deadly shot of eyes
   Shall search his faults who freedom's hope denies ;
Nor envious lips shall stint him gibe nor scorn,
Who filched the crown to which he was not born.

XCI.

" Who made thee more than us ? Thy acts of worth
   All by the hands of others thou hast done ;
O, man of many shifts ! thyself go forth,
   If that thou beest indeed Napoleon,
   In the brave battle prove by fire, upon
The foes of France thy right to bear that name,
And live or die the eldest born of Fame !

XCII.

" Terrible only to the hoodwinked French,
   Thou woman-slayer, robber of the night,
White-livered Corsican ! not thou would'st blench
   Though set o'er graves the bed of thy delight
   Safe, while our children's blood upbears thy might."
And the proud heart grew sore within him, stung
With words, the envenomed arrows of the tongue.

XCIII.

And Italy, that helped to build his glory,
  His creditor for blood yet unrepaid,
Seeks the lost thread of her immortal story,
  Whose end the world shall see, though **long delayed**:
  With hope unwavering, though oft betrayed,
She lifts her eyes toward him and makes demand:
What **woof** may fill the shuttle in his hand?

XCIV.

Hers by his bond, the Carbonaro's oath
  In youthful rashness sworn, now hedged with power
An Emperor spurns the unlawful contract, loth
  To bring to mind that past and evil hour;
  Dark brows of mystery and silence lower
On the false brother, and for broken faith
Appeal remains not from his doom of death.

XCV.

Orsini's arm falls short, yet 'neath the ban
  Of Heaven and earth he boasts his glorious aim:
" While vengeance burns, there shall not fail a man
  To shed thy blood, and mock at death and shame,
  A son of Italy! Dost ask my name?
OUR name is legion: clouds of living things
Darkening thy sun, with murther in their wings."

XCVI.

Shall Cæsar, like a recreant, stricken slave,
   Hold life on sufferance of another's will?
Better invoke the fortune of the brave,
   Go forth, and cast vile fear behind, until
   He come again in triumph, or fulfil
The dues of Glory by his fall, sublime
In victory, rather than the prey of crime!

XCVII.

Hence Discord bore his challenge to provoke
   'Gainst Hapsburg's might, the ordeal of the sword;
Fastening the blame for faith of treaties broke
   On the young heir of Empire, Austria's lord,
   Enticed by fatal wrath from honour's ward;
Within whose veins the warm and living flood
Boasts the pure drops of great Theresa's blood.

XCVIII.

The eagle's brood, untutored to endure
   The gall of insult, from his " pride of place"
Stoops headlong to the crafty fowler's lure;
   Down swoops the monarch of the Teuton race
   In arms on Italy!   Never to retrace
That first false step, nor by repentance bend
The course of ruin from its bitter end!

XCIX.

Lo, now, Italia's captive daughter waits[6]
   Heaven's signal, and in contemplation pale
Reads on a book till, thundering at her gates,
   Comes swift fulfilment of the poet's tale,
   How justice on this earth shall yet prevail :—
So to her sorrow-wounded breast may she
Take faith assured of glorious days to be.

C.

Lift up thine eyes, O Prisoner of Hope !
   Not dead art thou, but sleepest ; a higher sway
Than the mere will of Kaiser or of Pope
   Bursts through thy tomb, and bids thee rise this day
   A bride exulting, crowned with Freedom's ray,
That star long worshipped ere from heaven it fell,
Kindling thy torch with light unquenchable !

CI.

Put not your trust in Princes ! Italy
   Herself shall do and dare ! though France may boast
" From Alp to Adriatic be ye free
   By our good help"—oh ay, they count the cost
   Of barren victory such as on the host
Of iron men of Rome, too dearly won
Swart Hannibal, or Grecia's godlike son.[9]

CII.

Are these the men who dare not, though they would
  Act o'er again their fathers' deeds of wonder,
When a young giant rose to war, and stood
  On Lodi's bridge unharmed amidst the thunder?
  Will Fate be moved, once more to bring ye under
The sceptre of the Lion, whom she mocks,
Sold with the kiss of Fortune to the Fox?

CIII.

Too little valiant, though in counsel great,
  To earn the wages of a hero's work
In honour's gory field, yet spurred by Fate
  Through hills of carnage 'neath the horrid murk
  Of the thick cannon smoke, well may it irk
Some fibre in his heart to mark what sum
Of noble lives hath bought his masterdom!

CIV.

Magenta, Solferino! Fame doth greet
  Him conqueror on these fields, who present there
Tasted almost the anguish of defeat,
  Saved by the narrow 'vantage of a hair;
  So hath he 'scaped the fire—let him beware
The God of Battles' wrath, if e'er again
He call upon that dreadful name in vain!

CV.

Now Austria's star grows pale, and bright renown
   Is won by France in Italy's cause, with gift
Of fair Milan, the Lombards' Iron Crown,
   And many a league of goodly earth—best thrift
   Hath taught the Teuton in his strait to rift
The envied circlet of his diadem,
Bartered for days of respite gem by gem.

CVI.

So may Napoleon rest from weary labour,
   Beneath the laurel's shade; his glorious reign
Widens its borders o'er his grateful neighbour
   Raised to Italia's throne, while Gaul hath ta'en
   Of him fair lands betwixt the Alp and main,
Whose rivers feed the olive and the rose,
And spread o'er earth the riches of the snows.

CVII.

Yea, for an Emperor's greed, the aspiring king
   Must wear his crown debased with foul alloy,
Smile 'neath the burning brow that feels the sting
   Of shame within Ambition's dazzling toy;
   Resign the cradle of his race, Savoy,
And that bright lake, whose love-lit waters keep
God's lonely temple where their ashes sleep.[10]

CVIII.

There, dead for sorrow of the Austrian yoke,
   And cold in earth now alienate, the sire
From 'neath the tomb yet speaketh, to invoke
   Prayers of strange lips—and if the son require
   That life, and the full bent of his desire
On Italy's foes, how bitter is the cross
Of sweet revenge, bought dear at such a loss !

CIX.

Oh, rugged as the nurseling of the wolf,
   Show forth within the verge of living ken
Those grand old days when valour bridged the gulf
   'Twixt the young state and safety !—now as then
   The strong right hand bears rule ; even now do men
Seek in thy name an omen and a spell,
Shall strive with Fate, Victor Emmanuel !

CX.

To thee the oppressed of the earth impute
   Might to redress ; on thee the nations call
As erst on Jove's own son ; the golden fruit,
   Success for labour wrought, to thee doth fall ;
   Modena, Parma, and the pearl of all,
Florence, weave garlands for thy feet ; with these
Met in delight, thy new Hesperides !

CXI.

In thee is found such virtue as 'tis meet
    The keen marauder live by—to affront
With iron forehead injury, shame, defeat
    Of dearest effort, till misfortune's brunt
    Wear edgeless; constancy, by natural wont,
Commends thee and thy cause to men thy like,
Made to the occasion, as the sword to strike !

CXII.

So, smarting 'neath intolerable wrong,
    Swift Garibaldi, foe of " right divine,"
Brought thee a gift, the birthplace of sweet song,
    Parthenope, and joined his hand with thine
    'Gainst the Priest-king, whom weak men's fears en-
        shrine
I' the place of God o'er Italy, and he
Weighs on her neck, the Old Man of the Sea !

CXIII.

Steered by his aged hand, St. Peter's boat
    Puts off into the gale, perchance to ride
The seething waves and live—if man to float
    His frail-built craft may stay both time and tide,
    And check the swell of French Imperial pride :
If this may be, his scarlet robe worn old
Shall patch its rents with new-spun purple fold.

CXIV.

From Alp to Adriatic ! 'twas the word
   Of promise—the profession of the lip,
While to the sense the wavering heart demurred.
   Alas for Venice ! panting in the grip
   Of a strange lord, whose oars' abhorrèd dip
Into her married waters, coldly falls
Athwart the echoes of her gem-laid halls.

CXV.

Was this the virgin daughter of old Rome,
   Who fled her pleasant palaces to shun
A conqueror's touch, and made herself a home
   'Midst the wild waste of ocean ?   Lo, the Hun
   Luxuriates on her breast before the sun ;
Clothed with his rays and mellowed in his warmth
Her beauty doth corrupt the eye it charmeth.

CXVI.

How sunk to this ?   The Lady of the Isles,
   Soiled by the touch of soul-seducing gold,
Hearkened to great Napoleon, with smiles
   Of high-viced prostitution, bought and sold
   His, who or ere the embrace of sin grew cold
Had trucked her with the Austrian for surcease
Of contest, and dishonourable peace.

CXVII.

So fell the blast of Faliero's curse
   On them and on their children, in whose laws
Mercy was not—he dying, left a worse
   Reign of the viper's brood to avenge his cause :
   That severed head through ages speaks, which was
A Doge in Venice !   Living flesh must quail
O'er those shrunk features' agonising tale.[11]

CXVIII.

Wrong gendereth wrong—the next and nearest heir
   Of Empire's mightiest lord, his like, though less,
Wrought on the wind in labour to repair
   The irreparable evil done ; redress
   By man remains not for man's guiltiness ;
Let be the Hand that moves the wheels of time
To mete again the measure filled by crime !

CXIX.

Seven years, as days amidst the ages' sand,
   From Solferino to Sadowa led
The double-crested eagle—his last stand
   For empire, and from that day forth hath bled
   The deadly wound upon his second head ;
Struck down, but not by France ; another tore
The cloud-borne monarch from his height of soar.

CXX.

Lo, Austria, by the counsel of the fool,
   Joined hands with Prussia 'gainst the oppressèd Dane:
The more his guilt who makes himself a tool
   To grind another with the like sharp pain
   That galled his proper breast—the less his gain
Whose foul desires upon himself recoil,
Baulked of his due division of the spoil.

CXXI.

Thus in their mutual sin the root of strife
   Was laid 'twixt both these nations; thence sprang up
Quick the ill weed of hatred—by the knife
   The weaker shall be slain; or slowly sup
   More than death's sharpness in the bitter cup
Of shame-envenomed life—thy crowning woe,
O strong man, worsted by a stronger foe!

CXXII.

Louder than woman's wail the giant's cry
   Wrung forth by pain—the wild appeal for help
Broke from the Austrian in his agony:
   Who hears, who answers?—Not the Lion's whelp,
   Outroared to dumbness by the horrid yelp
Of faction's dogs, who watch him, tame to quell
His spirit with doubts and rising-up of hell.

F

CXXIII.

He hearken now, who summoned twice, held back
   From England all athirst for justice, fain
To guard the sacred roof from utter wrack
   Whence her own kings shall spring, to save the Dane!
   There struck the hour to seize and crush his bane,
And not in ineffectual prayers let pass
The day of honour where his safety was !

CXXIV.

No help in him, whose purpose-failing hand
   Toys nerveless from the scabbard to the hilt,
When need and hope cry out to grasp the brand :
   Forsaken Austria shall bear her guilt,
   Such quarrel suits not France—howe'er thou wilt
Name the defection—policy, caution, mere
Colours of art, to veil the blush of fear.

CXXV.

So, France unthanked, at last is Venice free ;
   Prussia hath risen to grant the priceless boon—
Liberty—as her gift ; amidst the sea
   The many isles rejoice—the bright lagoon
   Laughs jubilant in the undiminished noon ;
Such honour Prussia gains, not France, but hath
 Cause for the gathering storm-cloud of her wrath.

CXXVI.

Surely the passions in her bosom brood
  Fierce offspring, quickened by the blast of shame,
Whose pangs have wrought her till her fateful mood
  Brings forth the whirlwind and the thunder flame
  Upon her ravisher, who bartered, tame
Her glory with another. Coldly feed
The eyes their lust, beside ambition's greed.

CXXVII.

Another sting beyond France' proper wrong
  Devours her heart, deep cankering through the core :
A cry of wrath and pain is heard among
  The crownèd race of Europe ; from the shore
  Of the far-off New World goes up once more
The voice of blood, as when the curse of Cain
Avenged young Conradino, foully slain ![12]

CXXVIII.

Oh, child of Hapsburg ! Wherefore was the gift
  Of empire an enticement to decoy
Thee to thy fate ? rememberest not how swift
  Fell ruin on Constance' bright, heroic boy,
  When France usurped his birthright, to destroy ?
Like doomed shall Maximilian perish, in
Life's morning glory, for another's sin.

CXXIX.

Trite was the tale : how robbers in the West,
   By Europe's careless sufferance grown o'erbold,
Lording o'er land, and creek, and bay, infest
   Broad Mexico, corrupt ere while through gold :
   These France hath trampled, but to keep and hold
Her conquest, she hath need of some slight thing
Clothed with her power—the semblance of a king.

CXXX.

Therefore she wooes the brother second-born
   Of Austria with a throne ; the hand that bruised
An Emperor's heart, pleads softly to adorn
   His kinsfolk's brows with crowns ; nor, oft refused,
   Will take denial of the sceptre, used
To tempt a man, until he feel how sweet
The glittering bauble thrust beneath his feet.

CXXXI.

Oh, sweeter yet to woman !   Could his wife,
   Ambitious Charlotte, let cold scruples dim
The future's fiery draught, though 'twere her life
   Should buy her joy ?—She quaffed beneath the brim
   The maddening cup, then pressed it upon him,
Her husband—ah, God pity both, so young,
When 'cross their path the bait of death was flung !

CXXXII.

Was't not the folly of our mother Eve
  In bliss, to snatch perdition's fruit, mista'en
For greatness?   Nero's mother could believe
  The warning voice, yet will her son to reign
  Her murderer!   Oh, curse of woman's strain,
To thwart high heaven's decree, and set above
Man's earthly lot the idol of her love!

CXXXIII.

This one was fair, and gifted to subdue
  A doting husband's will: Imperial grace
Tempered her loftiness of nature, true
  To its high aim, the bent of Orleans' race;
  A father's darling, her sweet name, sweet face
Minded him of his love in other years—
England's lost Princess, mourned with many tears.[15]

CXXXIV.

The die is cast; of husband and of sire
  At last she wins their slow consent, o'ercome
By her proud spirit's one supreme desire,
  Severing each tender link of birth and home:
  Far from her pleasant lot content to roam
O'er the great sea 'neath sails of hope, unfurled
To Fortune's breezes toward an unknown world.

CXXXV.

Much praise of France and blessing of the Pope
    Speed the new Emperor's promise-laden keel
Toward Montezuma's seat ; the sandy rope
    Is fixed to bind it fast to ground, and heal
    Division 'mongst his people ; Christian zeal
Bidding him make thy mission good, or die,
Oh, Pio Nono, of the evil eye ![14]

CXXXVI.

Silent, that people met their lord, whose voice
    Should have confirmed his title : France forgot
Their will might baffle hers ; the Austrian buoys
    His heart with hope to efface the fraudful blot
    Fixed on his name, and win yet of them what
Kaiser nor Pope can give nor take away,
Man's free obedience to a righteous sway.

CXXXVII.

Deceived, beguiled to such attempt, as none
    Might bring to effect, that royal hand was set
To the stern labour France had left undone,
    Galled with her yoke and burthened with her debt ;
    Surety for her in gold and blood, he let
The fiery circle close before him, blind
Not to discern the consequence behind !

CXXXVIII.

Fierce the Columbian turns to bruise the heel
   Of Europe, ere she trample on his neck :
Fierce shall the sword repay him, till he feel
   Napoleon his master, at whose beck
   The new-enfeoffèd Prince, his tool and geck,
On each man ta'en in arms must execute
His death-doom, striking treason at the root.

CXXXIX.

It will not be—the hand that could enforce
   A friend to deeds of blood, makes no return
Of safety for the fetters of remorse
   Borne by that noble heart : the land doth spurn
   Her foreign lord, with those who bade him earn
Such measure to himself, and shall repay
Harsh judgment in the monarch of a day.

CXL.

France knows her fault, and ere it be too late,
   To save such honour as her arms have won,
Forsakes the land and him, infatuate,
   Resolved to hold his useless struggle on ;
   Who scorns, at bidding of Napoleon,
To quit some few in whom he hath found faith,
So bideth still with them, for life or death.

CXLI.

Beseiged, shut in, 'twixt sword and famine, hemmed
   By sure destruction's narrowing circle round,
Sold to his foes, and at their will condemned
   By the mock tribunal their rage hath found
   To pour his life-blood on that alien ground,
In face of Europe's lords and kings, because
They sought to tread down free Columbia's laws.

CXLII.

He fell beneath the murdering bullet shower,
   The noblest of them, while they stood far off,
Struck dumb before the horrors of that hour :
   And no man dared to utter taunt or scoff
   'Mong that strange people, when they saw him doff
The garment of mortality, as 'twere
To robe in marriage vesture, white and fair.

CXLIII.

Used by Napoleon, as the drowning wretch
   Grasps at a straw to stay him, sinking deep
Beneath the floods that mock his desperate catch—
   Flung back in agony that will not keep
   The hold that failed it—when our age shall sleep,
Glory's faint ripple on the stream of time
Shall mark that life, too early crushed by crime.

CXLIV.

Accursèd was thy sacrifice, O fool,
  To merchandise for respite with the surge
Of man's waked wrath, uprisen to sweep thy rule
  From earth's fair face; those mighty waters scourge
  The rocks, thy narrow refuge, on the verge
Of ruin—would'st for power's abuse atone,
By yielding all to save thyself alone?

CXLV.

Thou would'st, but mayest not : lo ! the dreadful rush
  Of people, the indignant feet of men—
The clamour of the lip—the withering blush
  Shame prints on every Frenchman's forehead—when
  Suppliant to thee again, and yet again,
Charlotte, the wretched wife, appeals : who dare
Look coldly on her frenzy of despair?

CXLVI.

Not now for power—for life—his life—she begs
  Help from thy hand ; no icy, hard rebuff
Moves her proud lips from tasting to the dregs
  Humiliation's poisoned cup—too rough
  Thy touch that crushed her soul with grief enough
To slay—but fire and strength of youth deny
The last, best hope of misery—to die.

G

CXLVII.

She lives, and he is dead—horrible thought
  To love, that gulf of silence should divide
Their passion-mingled spirits; her's, o'erfraught,
  Bore not its burthen, reason swerved aside
  From conflict with the foe too hard to bide,
Brain-racking madness—till her senseless moan
Might melt to tears of blood the heart of stone.

CXLVIII.

Hers by the bond, nor life nor death can sever—
  That glorious form her eyes shall see no more
Comes back among his own to rest for ever:
  The waters of the Adriatic bore
  His body, piercèd by the bloody door
That gave the winged soul passage—bore him past
Their fairy home of joy, too dear to last.[15]

CXLIX.

People and kings, Imperial brother, all
  Paid him the due of tears—but no revenge:
Only the hour that shuddered at his fall
  Loomed darkly in the shadow of a change
  Over the spirit of France, turned fierce and strange
Upon her lord; the universal hiss
Shoots in his ear: " Napoleon has done this !"

CL.

Now is the day at hand when France, too long
    Divided 'gainst herself, shall cast the blame
For all on him, and by her union strong
    To spurn the yoke of fear, of him shall claim
    Count of the deeds committed in her name :
Shame, hot and bitter, hath she drunk like water,
Till her thirst burneth in desire of slaughter.

CLI.

Ay, this last hope yet tempts him, to make good
    In arms his title to the Imperial crown.
France will not waive her choice, confirmed in blood,
    If power and will avail him to cast down
    The rising star of Prussia's young renown.
He asks her, jealous, " Shall another be
First nation in the world, in place of thee ?"

CLII.

Yet war's dread trumpet breathed no certain sound
    With human passion, till a voice of heaven
Lodged in the bosom of a man was found,
    Proclaimed Infallible : who most hath striven
    'Gainst him shall yield, or perish unforgiven ;
Men shall fall down and worship him as God,
Who moves or stays time's progress with his nod.

CLIII.

So, in His name who made the inviolate mind
   In His own image, issues the decree
To fetter every thought of man, and blind
   His inward light—the Teuton deemed him free
   To weld his mighty race in unity,
One people, though of divers creeds, their band
Of brotherhood, strong love of Fatherland :

CLIV.

Uncounselled dreamer !   Rome hath spoke the word,
   And the proud fabric of thy hope shall fall
And wither 'neath her curse : hath she not stirred
   Old strife between the German and the Gaul ?
   And France in arms makes answer to the call ?
Woe to the land which lying prophets move
To wrath and murder for the law of love !

CLV.

Woe to the Prince who yields himself the slave
   Of war's fell demon, though he hate the cause :
Rome claims her due, remembering him who gave
   Fair France to be his leman ; yet there was
   Remorse within his breast had bid him pause,
Could he have wrestled with that stronger will
Whose 'hest the loathful spirit must fulfil !

CLVI.

Yea, and an influence keener and more human
   Strove through the wife's caress, the mother's fear
With pity in his soul—oh, heart of woman,
   Wed to thy dignities at cost so dear;
   Bitter should be thy life of exile here,
Envenomed by the thought how many a one
Were happy, had'st thou never borne a son !

CLVII.

Ah, little warned of late remorse to come,
   Wil't break the silence of the world's repose,
And mar the spell that kept it, listening, dumb,
   For war's full diapason of all woes
   To miserable men ?   All ready glows
The match beside the train, the mutual ire
Of race, a spark may kindle into fire.

CLVIII.

Eye fixed on eye, the Teuton and the Celt
   Cross in their paths; with high, o'erbearing hand
One carries insult unexpressed, yet felt
   Quick by the other, hot to make his stand
   'Gainst the rude stretch of insolent command :
A word, a gesture shall provoke renewal
Of hate to achieve their interrupted duel.

CLIX.

France angered, deems the quarrel thrust upon her
    Wilily by the foe, who bideth cool
Till some hard precept in the code of honour,
    As written in the Bible of the fool,
    Urge her in wrath no policy can school
To stake her all in war's delusive game,
'Gainst uncomputed odds of loss and shame.

CLX.

Now these new troubles unto France begin
    From Spain once more, as ever it befel ;
With great debate 'mongst Princes, who shall win
    The vacant throne of banished Isabel :
    Till one by one the sons of Kings repel
The borrowed honours of another's seat
Where prudence doubts, and virtue fears defeat.

CLXI.

At length the purpose holds to set a branch
    Of younger growth from Prussia's royal house
In Spanish soil :—in opposition staunch
    France bars his claim, whose dignities arouse
    Her jealous fury : Prussia's King allows
Her plea —commands his kinsman to forbear
The proffered throne, but farther hath no care.

CLXII.

Enough to pluck the arrow from the wound
   Of pride, where yet the poisoned barb remains,
To atone the past, and hold his faith unbound
   For time to come : the Monarch's soul disdains
   Question beyond—while busy rumour feigns
Rebuffs, shames, mutual insults, such as are
Both nations' curse—the bitter cause of war.

CLXIII.

The deed is done : Napoleon, evil starred,
   Gives to his people what they would, and pale
As doom goes forth among them : cold and hard
   His eye, whose bend o'erawes them, till he fail :
   Moving triumphant in their midst, all hail
Him now ; even those who hate him swell the din,
The maddening shout of thousands, "To Berlin!"

CLXIV.

"War, war ! our sword is sharp, our heart is light :
   Sons of the men of Jena, are not ye
France' strong right arm made ready for the fight ?
   Such legions, eldest born of victory,
   Ne'er hath she had, and ne'er again shall see
Such chance, if she let slip the happy time !"
False promise, fatal blunder, worse than crime !

CLXV.

Surely he falls, with strong delusion fed
    By lying flatterers, even the same who built
His throne on sand : the spirits of the dead
    Press on them to break short beneath the hilt
    Their swords, yet red with unatonèd guilt :
Himself, at odds with sore disease and pain,
Leads forth the hosts he ne'er shall bring again !

CLXVI.

Defrauded in the measure of his strength,
    The lesson is to learn how little worth
His empire's tools, brought face to face at length
    In battle with the Genius of the North
    Uprisen in slow rage, and bodied forth
In stern array of men : one heart, one soul
    From monarch unto peasant, stirs the whole !

CLXVII.

So nature orders her resistless force
    In Nilus' waters, when the melting snows
O'ercharge the secret fountains of his source,
    And in his bed Nyanza's lake o'erflows :
    Nor strength nor cunning is in man t' oppose
His branchless spreading current, unwithstood
Till Egypt's land lies buried 'neath the flood.

CLXVIII.

Strong in unswerving purpose, they break through
  Napoleon's wild defence—well skilled to find
Their vantage—and with numbers, aye too few,
  He met their shock, as three 'gainst one combined:
  Thus staked his all, and kept no hope behind ;
Nor was the tender youth of his fair boy
Witheld from sport with war, as with a toy.

CLXIX.

One moment, mocked with colour of success
  By Fortune's scorn, some impulse bade him shrink
From the sharp contest—'twas not fear !—nathless
  He wanders up and down upon the brink
  Of ruin, ere beneath its waves he sink ;
While in mid-current of defeat, Douay
With death upon a rock, casts off dismay.

CLXX.

On Geisberg's height, from August dawn till noon
  He strove, then looked upon the battle lost,
Turned, slew his faithful steed, and sought like boon,
  Quick end of pain, the prize he craved the most:
  On, with the remnant of his baffled host
He rushed ; they asked him " Whither ?"—" To the
  foe !"
He cried, and sought and found a mortal blow.

H

CLXXI.

A little band yet stood upon the field
   In arms : again, and yet again, till e'en
They spurned the conqueror's grace, when urged to yield,
   Who bare them down, but spared to slay—fourteen
   They counted, left of hundreds : well I ween
Friedrich, the Royal chieftain, found that day
Some stuff in France to cope with on his way !

CLXXII.

Away upon the scent ! Let sound a mort
   Over the stricken prey, then on !—Well thrives
Thy hot pursuit upon the hills of Wörth,
   Grim huntsman, War, whose chase are human lives !
   There brought to bay, how fiercely, vainly strives
The o'erspent deer thy pack hath set upon
Magenta's hero, noble MacMahon !

CLXXIII.

Yea, and within the self-same evil hour
   Hath Thor brought down his hammer at Spiecheren,
With godlike strength of blows, to break the power
   Of Celtic fury : he hath bent him, stern,
   To climb that pass, though step by step he earn
His way through blood, till slaughtered thousands heap
His gory passage up that hard-held steep !

CLXXIV.

Mark how the bravest sons of France have died,
  The soldier and his chief together there
Locked in embrace : the earth shall not divide
  Their ashes, nor despoil the hand that bare
  Safe to the grave a lock of woman's hair :
The hero's heart can yield but dust to dust—
Sealed to eternity its love and trust !

CLXXV.

Oh, knew they but the coming sorrows, blest
  Beyond the living those who timely fell,
Their faces to the foe ; woe worth the rest,
  Such tale of shame, dismay, and loss to tell !
  Then France rose up, and with the hate of hell
Turned on her monarch, then her curse received
His word of comfort, " All may be retrieved !"

CLXXVI.

What yet was left him he gave up, supreme
  Only in misery now : another hand
Must guide his armies, for he knows men deem
  Himself unworthy of the chief command :
  A woman in the counsels of the land
Shall fill his seat—could he propitiate
By sacrifice of all the wrath of fate !

CLXXVII.

One impulse yet, the instinct of dear life
　　Drives him towards Paris—like the hunted fox
Fled to his lair—that refuge, friend and wife
　　Madly forbid him : thus the woodsman blocks
　　The access where the wretch would earth, and baulks
His last poor double, ere he pant beneath
The mangling fangs, and sate their lust in death.

CLXXVIII.

If such the inevitable, shall it skill
　　What evil counsel adding to his fault
Hasten the issue?　Seeming wisdom still
　　Bids him divert afar the fierce assault,
　　Lest Paris' walls be violate—pause or halt
Might yet ward off to some less vital part
The point of peril from the nation's heart.

CLXXIX.

Within the maiden walls of Metz, Bazaine,
　　Now arbiter of France, her armies' chief,
Dwells safe no longer; better might he gain
　　Deliv'rance by his sword than wait relief
　　And perish in expectance : as the thief
Snatches the swift occasion of the night,
He sets his legions on the path of flight :

CLXXX.

His aim, to reach the rallying ground, Chalons,
  Ere he join battle with the Norse, to band
His strength unbroken there, with MacMahon's
    Unheartened host, and thus to take their stand
    'Gainst the too vigilant foe—ah, vainly planned
Hope to elude his meshes! no resource
Availeth, but the last appeal to force.

CLXXXI.

Three armies in his reins, the German king
  With Steinmetz and the Red Prince, from the South
Catches their flying columns on the wing,
    Drives up and smites them flankways, nor alloweth
    Room for their westward march—the cannon's mouth
Bore full upon their hastening ranks, and mowed
Dread harvest either side the narrow road:

CLXXXII.

The road, with trees and clustered hamlets bound,
  The key to Paris! from the hills of Görze
To Vionville, the shifting French took ground;
    And ere the foe could put them to the worse,
    The soil of France grew rich with many a corse:
Who 'scapes the mitrailleuse' close hail shall feel
The crash of charging horse, the chill of steel!

CLXXXIII.

Night fell upon their wrath: no martial tones
    Of Luther's hymn nor Watch upon the Rhine
Thrill through the darkness, but the long, low moans
    Of pain and agony : with eyes divine
    The stars look down compassionate—incline
Some nearer friend, O Thou who mad'st the skies
Toward the lone pillow where the warrior dies !

CLXXXIV.

Man beareth aid, and woman; they had missed her
    Upon that slaughter-field, help of the lorn,
Past comfort else ! The angels call her sister
    Who sheds on misery's night the smile of morn,
    Sweet pity's heavenly glow ; in such are born,
While yet on earth, the immortal seeds of love
Whose perfect flower shall crown the blest above.

CLXXXV.

Fair rose the morrow's sun above the wood
    Where mingling armies strove unseen ; a taint
Floats on the air, the sickening scent of blood
    Points where the wretch, too weary for complaint,
    Hath borne his pain till ebbing life beat faint,
Soothed by desire of death, that friend indeed
Unsought by man till such dire, utmost need.

CLXXXVI.

A **son** of England tendeth to his **rest**[16]
  Yon bleeding chieftain of the Imperial guard ;
His hand yet grasps the medals on **his breast**,
  His lips bequeath that friend his shattered sword
  In memory **of** him—while a whispered word
Breathes forth **the** gallant spirit's prayer, set free
By that last effort, " Bury these with me !"

CLXXXVII.

Yet some shall live : lo where **the ground is red**
  Beneath her shadow's cool, the weeping birch,
Soft lady of the woods, bends down her head ;
  Nor vainly human pity speeds the search,
  Till tent and lazaret and village church
Teem and o'erflow with wreck of mangled forms,
By healing care delivered from the worms.

CLXXXVIII.

Scarce might they pause from strife one day ; Bazaine
  Retires upon the right and forms his front
Wedgewise upon the hills that gird the plain
  Round Metz the maid, to bear against the brunt
  Of battle, and break through : beyond his **wont**
He veils resolve in silence ; should he fail,
His blood-bought honours are a bygone tale.

CLXXXIX.

Again 'tis night o'er earth, and through the still
　Of darkness, and the sacred sleep of care
Pierces the note of warning : trumpets shrill,
　To trumpets answering on the midnight air,
　The call to arms; both hosts can scarce forbear
Their last encounter, till the morning light
Renew their spirits to the bitter fight.

CXC.

Prompt as the summons flies from camp to camp
　The German is afield—earth quails beneath
Their countless numbers' closely measured tramp,
　Evolving northwards in a mighty wreath,
　Recurvous where the eye of guidance seeth
A break amidst the hills of slaughtering fire,
Where the unyielding French their powers retire.

CXCI.

If haply there they prove assailable,
　The Red Prince' thousands set across their course
Cut off retreat towards Paris—to repel
　Them pressing on ere these have reached, the Norse,
　Quickly resolving, casts a charge of horse
Upon their batteries' hottest fire, to die
Holding the pass for coming victory.

CXCII.

Lo now their lances, like the beams of day,
   Peep glittering o'er the brow of yonder hill;
Now from their throats breaks forth a wild hurrah,
   The cry of dauntless hearts, a sound to thrill
   Their chargers rushing on to death—they kill
The cannoneers and seize the guns; then fall
Like stones built on a rock, a flawless wall,

CXCIII.

A barrier in the passage of the French,
   Till from the north the cannon's nearer boom
Tells of the Red Prince hard at hand to wrench
   The fruit of triumph from destruction's womb:
   Within the opposing lines he hath found room
To conquer, and the battle wind breathes hot
Upon the wood-clad slopes of Gravelotte.

CXCIV.

The mitrailleuse' harsh whirr, another voice
   Added to death, rolls clear above the blast
Of shot and shell, through age-long hours that poise
   Fate's equal balance—ere the cloud be past,
   And either foe enduring to the last
Outlive the **fury** of that dark Simoom,
The dust lies deep o'er many a hero's tomb.

CXCV.

Once and again the Prussian ranks advance
    Up the steep chasm where their comrades died :
Once more and yet again the men of France
    Slaying and slain, the fierce attack abide ;
    Not these alone the issue shall decide ;
Germania still pours forth her living stream
Of myriads, like the vision of a dream.

CXCVI.

Up from the south and o'er the swift Moselle
    They wound their way by night, and deftly clomb
Hill, rock, and steep ravine, until their spell
    Of war's grim work was called ; then issuing from
    Ognon's thick forest, where the death-winged bomb
Broke on their covert, four hours long unrolled
Their coil of strength, in Python fold o'er fold.

CXCVII.

Dark spots lay thick upon that serpent trail
    Where torment-writhen flesh, bestained with gore,
Fell on the way—nor wound nor death could quail
    The huge advancing monster, on he tore
    Through fire and blood, and wound him round and o'er
His prey, till 'neath his fangs they turn, they rush
In frantic hope to 'scape his mangling crush.

CXCVIII.

Then Prussia's crest stooped low; almost was lost
  The priceless ground, disputed inch by inch
All that long day, at such unmeasured cost
  Of mortal anguish; than at last might flinch
  Strength, if not will in peril's sharpest pinch:
Then calmly rose amid the battle smoke
The aged warrior king, Germania's oak:

CXCIX.

No tremors move that high heroic soul;
  That royal hand hath ta'en its foremost share
I' th' hard day's labour: master of the whole,
  He kens the point amidst the compass where
  Fate's needle quavers; soon he brings to bear
New strength upon the issue of the hour:
Close thrust of steel and fire-borne iron shower

CC.

On with a mighty shout and beat of drum
  Down the ravine they rush, and up the height
Hurl themselves on the foe! Still on they come,
  Still flash on flash the stream of fire glows bright,
  Then sinks in distance 'neath the thickening night:
The Gaul must yield, on every side borne in
The road his vanquished thousands died to win.

CCI.

Slow he retreats in anger through the dusk :
    Like as the hunted boar escaped unslain,
With signs of battle in his shattered tusk,
    Foul with rent flesh, in many a clotted stain,
    His own and others' gore, oft turns again
On his pursuers, ere within his lair
He eat his heart in sharpness of despair.

CCII.

Night wore away in pain—another sun
    Bore witness to the haughty Teuton's boast ;
Bazaine o'erthrown sustains a cause foredone,
    Close blocked, together with his countless host,
    Where they must yield or perish !   Yet almost
Too dear-bought seemed the joy, when morning shed
Light on the moveless faces of the dead :

CCIII.

Light on the living heaps of mangled flesh
    Scarce left the form of man !   Yet unto those
Unfailing love pours forth her balm afresh,
    Sweetening the taste of death : there one, who knows
    Sorrow her old familiar, wildly goes
From group to group, imploring sign or word
To tell where lies the body of her lord. [17]

CCIV.

Save for those two, by love made one in heart,
  Had Maximilian died without a friend
Proof against fate, nor ever would depart
  That true wife from her husband, till the end
  Through flood and fire she followed him, to spend
In helpful toil her golden days of youth ;
Cold now the lips that should reward her truth.

CCV.

Woe to the conqueror ! All through Fatherland
  This day of sorrow doth one home remain
Where cruel death hath spared to lay his hand ?
  Hush the loud shout of triumph, nor profane
  The broken spirit's sacred hours of pain ;
What profits victory to those who mourn
'Neath life's dull load, of all life's joys forlorn ?

CCVI.

Woe to the conquered ! How should flesh endure
  Ills that in mortal language have no name ?
O France ! thy misery is wrought past cure,
  Thy heart-wound deep, that bartered blood for fame
  To loss of both ; wilt cast thy bitter blame
For all on him, whose hand hath never swerved
From doing thy desire, too blindly served !

CCVII.

Again the voice of wisdom at his side
   Urged his return to Paris, thence to ward
Destruction off; the City in her pride
   And fury fiercer than the wounded pard
   Turns on her keeper, if he fail to guard
Her offspring ;—and again he made reply—
" Dead or victorious "—till the hour passed by.

CCVIII.

And MacMahon, for he was high of mind,
   Rejected not the Emperor's wild appeal
To help Bazaine ; so rushed on loss, not blind
   To consequence ; 'twas all devouring zeal
   For honour bade him prove he could not feel
Envy's base stings, nor doubt nor hesitate
To save a rival chief, self immolate !

CCIX.

With hope 'gainst hope he nerves his hand to gather
   The broken remnants wasted by defeat,
Though the heart melt within him, as they wither
   Like snow-wreaths smitten by the morning heat :
   And these are all that France hath left to meet
Victorious Friedrich, these alone dispute
The pass toward Paris 'gainst his hot pursuit.

CCX.

These from her walls the Imperial city spurns,
　Till Metz be saved with her—or both at once,
Or neither, so she wills it—northwards turns
　The host, by hills and forests of Argonnes,
　And o'er the Meuse' swift waters, Mac Mahon's
Passage may yet be won—if then Bazaine
Break forth and meet him through the circling chain,

CCXI.

They two may rescue France!—Too swift the feet,
　Too keen the brain that follows up their track!
As wisdom bade him, from the untasted sweet
　Of conquest, royal Friedrich turneth back;
　Nor pauseth he nor murmureth to slack
His arm stretched forth on Paris, and forego
The present, for the future's surer blow.

CCXII.

Left of the Meuse he hasteth on, before
　The tell-tale winds be 'ware of his intent;
Sightless as death, the Saxon levies pour
　Along the Eastern bank, adroitly bent
　To seize the points of passage, and prevent
The advancing French; while close round Metz through all
　　through all
The Red Prince stays, to hold Bazaine in thrall.

CCXIII.

Had MacMahon conveyed his powers beyond
  The stream, and onwards with unbated haste
For life or death, ere fear dissolved the bond
  Of prompt obedience, held the distance placed
  'Twix him and his pursuers!—Wo the waste
Of golden hours, till days to weeks have spun,
In lingering essays at a task undone!

CCXIV

Laggard and mutinous, too late they reach
  The hopeful river, where their enemies
Met them unwary of attack : at each
  Bend of the stream, new clouds of marksmen rise,
  With wingèd death and horror of surprise;
Some ambush from each covert of the wood
Breaks, where they dreamed of passage unwithstood.

CCXV.

In battle with the spirit of the North
  Their own heart's fears have scattered them, like sheep
Deaf to their shepherd's voice; the wolf goes forth
  Among their wandering flocks no hand may keep,
  Huddling them onwards, a disordered heap
Toward their last stronghold, hateful with the ban
Of ancient curses, evil-famed Sedan.

CCXVI.

Yet one resource was left them, that last day
  Of August, had their silent ranks defiled
Retreating by the sole yet open way,
  Upon Mezières for Paris—hope-beguiled,
  Napoleon stayed them, but the Imperial child
Of France departs from him ; while lives his boy
This world hath something yet can give him joy !

CCXVII.

Fate-blinded, he awaits the day of strife
  With the strong kings of nations, unaware
Of the destroying angel with them ; life
  Remains, and with it hope, nor will he spare
  The wasted, pain-wrought frame must serve him there
To stake on the issue of this one last chance
Left to redeem the agony of France !

CCXVIII.

That sun arose as other suns, September's
  First morning—when the mists before his light
Were lifted up and scattered, France remembers
  How all around the city stood in sight
  The gathered myriads of Germania's might,
With whom shall Frenchmen, ere they yield, have striven
Through twelve long deathful hours, from dawn till even.

K

CCXIX.

Foremost fell MacMahon, ill-fated chief,
  Struck down beneath the shell-storm; bleeding, wan,
They bore him from the field, with shame and grief
  Worse stung than by his wound: Napoleon
  Sought death and found it not, till all was gone,
And pent within Sedan, the hell-borne shower
Crushed out his heart beneath a conqueror's power.

CCXX.

Then gallant Wimpffen raised a desperate cry:
  "Men, close around your Emperor, we'll cut through
Yon ranks a way to liberty, or die!
  Would ye be ta'en like sheep?"—Alas, too few
  Would dare the deed! Then soldiers rose and slew
Their chiefs, and laid their murders on the man
Cursed by two names, December and Sedan!

CCXXI.

Then to the death-girt hosts of France he gave
  His last commandment; by his sovereign right,
To cease the useless carnage, caused them wave
  Above their battered gates the banner white,
  Whose folds must redden ere they stay the fight,
And meet response: "we hold you at our will
To absolute surrender, or we kill!"

CCXXII.

" Gunners se'en hundred by our pieces stand,
  The match upon the touch hole ; you are all
As dust within the hollow of our hand !"
  O night of shame and horror !   Such o'er Gaul
  Hath never darkened, since Alesia's fall
'Neath Roman Cæsar's arms : Louisa's son [18.]
Great honour of Napoleon's heir hath won.

CCXXIII.

Was't not her spirit bade the victor spare
  Her injurer's race, when vengeance came from God
For wrongs her queenly heart assayed to bear,
  And broke i' the effort?   Lower than the clod,
  Napoleon, envying the earth he trod
In strong desire of death, yet loth to die,
Might move compassion of his enemy !

CCXXIV.

Had he but dared the worst, to purchase peace
  For France, and ta'en upon himself alone
The burthen of his people !   Though surcease
  Of War, he deemed must consummate his own
  Defeat, and bar his offspring from the throne
He sinned to make secure—had he done this,
More than the conqueror's nobleness were his !

CCXXV.

Not so ; but steeped in obloquy to th' lips
    He passeth to captivity ; with him
His snarèd army suffereth eclipse
    Of fame, and as his day-star waxeth dim,
    France feels Invasion's cancer creep from limb
To body, toward her heart ; the fretted sore
Draining her life within its festering core.

CCXXVI.

Madly she turns upon the weaker half
    And powerless hand that grasped the reins of state,
Unwitting of the fiery car : a laugh
    Of base-souled churls pursues the Emperor's mate,
    Hurled from her seat of pride, to satiate
The evil passions of that evil time,
When woman wrought with man in blood and crime.

CCXXVII.

So beautiful, so mighty !   Is there no man
    In her great fall abideth true and fast,
Her friend indeed ?   Oh ! blinded will of woman,
    To chide the Italian King, when fain to cast
    His lot with hers, and serve her at the last :
" Let Paris yield to Prussia," answered she,
" Ere Rome to Italy !" —And this shall be,

CCXXVIII.

The other notwithstanding! That self-same
   September day saw Paris closèd in,
Engirt by iron men, and her whose name
   Is mystery, the mother of earth's sin,
   Cast down by him, who dared her curse to win
Man's freedom ; and the heavens shall echo one
Cry o'er both cities: Fallen is Babylon!

CCXXIX.

Italia una ! This our age fulfils
   The vision, clear to Dante's Prophet ken, [19.]
When she who sitteth on the seven hills
   Wantoned with kings and bought the souls of men :
   Lift up your voice in wailing for her ; when
The child of golden hope, immortal fame,
Atones Canosa's memories of shame ! [20.]

CCXXX.

Like as the lords of Asia's wide dominions
   When the fleet deer before their arrow flies,
Launch in pursuit on unresisted pinions
   The lightning wingèd monarch of the skies : [21.]
   He stoops upon the prey—the hot blood dyes
His talons ; fast they hold with maddening smart,
While his sharp beak rends out the quivering heart :

CCXXXI.

So William bade the chieftains of the Norse
   His messengers, go forth on eagles' wings
To cleave the breast of France in twain, and force
   Submission from her dire extreme ; he wrings
   A limb from her fair body, ere he brings
His legions in Imperial triumph home :
A king of men hath spurned the curse of Rome !

CCXXXII.

And France hath seen her queenly diadem
   In blood and ashes cast away ; the harm
Her conqueror spared her, is achieved by them
   Her bosom nursed ; their parricidal arm
   Hath marred her loveliness that once could charm
Men to forget the bonds of home and birth ;
The marvel and delight of all the earth !

CCXXXIII.

And yet for her is hope—the noble word
   Hath passed a Frenchman's lips : "Our great
      revenge [22.]
Should be upon ourselves."—If she hath erred
   Through blinded love of her false gods, a change
   Shall pass upon her spirit, bright and strange
Beyond ambition's wildest dreams,—the beauty
Of life and death wrought out in truth by duty !

CCXXXIV.

She bears her sorrows : let the nations take
  The example, and avoid the bitter doom :
May France receive, may England ne'er forsake
  The light from heaven enkindled midst the gloom
  Of misery, the blackness of the tomb :
So shall her glory, ere it pass away
Blend with the dawn of everlasting day !

ODE ON THANKSGIVING DAY.

FEBRUARY 27th, 1872.

I.

Lo, now, while England, listening from afar
The struggle of the nations, waiting calm
Fate's verdict, and the issue of the war
'Twixt light and chaos, gathers of the palm
No bloody harvest; but with sovereign balm
Of human pity, never shed in vain,
Bears part through kindness in another's pain;

II.

Within her shores is heard a voice of wail,
For her own woe—the heavy hand of death
Presses on her belovèd Prince, and pale,
The monarch and her people sink beneath
The impending doom : one expectation stayeth
The pulse of every heart ; one bitter cry
Bursts from each lip in common agony.

L

III.

And sound of prayer and heaven-persuading tears
To Thee, oh Father! rises from all lands
Where'er our language names Thee; hopes and fears
Cling to the life that trembles in Thy hands:
Ay, where the Parsee dimly understands
Thy power and presence, to the God of Fire
Goes up from India's plain our heart's desire.

IV.

And from the sacred s ones of Israel
Burns in the tender melody of sighs
The glorious, fearful Name no lip may tell;
Knit with this Christian land by sorrow's ties
Jerusalem weepeth; nor wilt Thou despise
Her broken harp's last murmuring, to move
Compassion of Thine everlasting love.

V.

Make not a desolation and a curse
In England, 'midst the Royal stem of Kings;
Leave not a people shepherdless, to worse
Than tyranny, the mock of baser things
Crept into light, when anarchy upsprings
To snatch the unguarded sceptre, given a prey
To factions, harbingers of power's decay!

VI.

Smite not our flower of strength in manhood's pride,
Whom we have seen, when youth's desire was won,
The sweetest rose of earth, his chosen bride,
With wedded love crowned glorious as the sun :
Far be the night from day so fair begun !
Thou Lord of Life, call back Thy message, save
The young, the happy, from the cruel grave !

VII.

What voice was silent ? even mine, the least,
Could pierce Thy heavens—oh Thou, All-wise, All-good,
Who knewest the heart that trusted Thee, nor ceased
To hope, when hope was not—O Father, could
Death pass from him, that not in widowhood
His love should mourn, his orphans' tender years
With unavailing anguish fill Thine ears !

VIII.

Mercy hath triumphed : hearkening our despair,
The parting spirit pauses at the gate
Of the dark vale—turns back, compelled by prayer
From the great silence, unrevealèd fate
Decreed for dust—new days of health await
The grave's devoted, set before our eyes
Restored by Him who bade the dead arise.

IX.

Him shall the glory of the living praise,
Gladness and joy of heart break forth and sing
His highest gift, heaven-conquering pain, to raise
Man's spirit on affliction's fiery wing
Above the stars ;—so England's Prince shall bring
Again the days of England's old renown :
Made worthy through the cross to wear the crown.

Ode ON THE MARRIAGE OF THE DUKE OF EDINBURGH AND THE GRAND DUCHESS MARIE ALEXANDROVNA.

I.

Peace be on earth !   Harsh note of war, be dumb,
 The night of ignorance and hate hath ceased :
Now to our shores a gentle guest doth come,
 The lady of the nations' marriage feast :
 Like morning light arisen in the East
To heal her people's strife with alien lands,
And knit our hearts in kindness' mutual bands.

II.

Daughter of Scythian monarchs, hail ! Fair bride
 Led captive to the Islands of the sea
By love, the mighty conquerer ; in thy pride
 Of youth and grace Imperial, thou shalt be
 Anchored on England's breast, hope's argosy
Won by our Sailor Prince ; with dearer prize
Never hath victory's pomp enriched our eyes !

III.

Nor lightly was the bloodless conquest earned,
　　In pleasure's race to wile an idle day
Our English Alfred bears a heart that yearned
　　To tread rough labour's honorable way :
　　Meetly home bliss the mariner shall repay,
Brooding o'er stormy seas through many a night
Thoughts iron-constant to his soul's delight.

IV.

Well proved that royal heart to mock at fear
　　Of darker peril than the stroke of war :
Ay, when the Assassin's stealthy aim touched near
　　Its citadel of life, more baleful far :
　　Of mettle such as Alfred's heroes are,
Such worth of manhood in his youth hath shone
As dove-eyed beauty loves to look upon.

V.

Lo, to the Northern Cæsar's halls he came
　　No stranger, in a wooer's gentle guise,
To spell earth's dearest word, a husband's name.
　　In the soft mirrors of his lady's eyes :
　　Not unfamiliar there such tender ties
Where blooms in sweetness 'midst the winter snows
A sister flower to Denmark's royal rose.

VI.

Seabound Crimea saw their time of love
  Glide blissful 'midst the gardens of the vine ;
There both to either's first affections clove,
  Blent heart in heart in unison divine,
  Close as the springing shoots their branches twine :
Rich as their promise, youth enamoured sips
The wine of life from timid virgin lips.

VII.

Bear back the tale, ye many sounding waves,
  Of love's soft triumph to Britannia's shore ;
Joy stirs the heroic dust of British graves
  Hallowed in Russian earth, that evermore
  Those young hearts' living freshness bloometh o'er
The evil days gone by of strife and pain,
Cossack 'gainst Saxon, ne'er to come again !

VIII.

Sons of the North, twin giants ! hath the world
  Power to oppose your strength combined as one
While side by side your standards float unfurled ?
  What warlike pageantry beneath the sun
  Shall match that sight, until his course be done ?
Far as his beams shall stretch from age to age
The future of your glorious heritage !

I.

Peace be on earth! the weary time hath rest:
In two hearts' love, two nations shall be blest:
Our eyes have opened on a happier day,
The lion and the bear like lambkins play.

II.

Fair Princess, who forsakest for another
Thy sire's Imperial breast, thy weeping mother,
May love draw down young spirits from heaven to earth,
And children's tongues make music on thy hearth!

III.

Prince of the ocean-empire! words are vain
To ease thy people's heart, o'erfraught with rain
Of tender prayers on million lips, to move
Rich showers of blessings on thee from above!

Leæna: an Elegy.

I.

Night thickens round, and desolation is
   Within me, like the frost-bound earth's decay;
My love, my love! in such an hour as this
   Thy spirit, angel-guarded, passed away.

II.

The leafless elm trees 'neath the weeping sky
   Steeped their bare heads in heavy drops of woe;
The soughing wind made moan for thee,—while I—
   I knew it not—expected not the blow.

III.

Why, why was I not there? thy head had lain
   Pillowed in love's own sweetness on my breast:
One word had more than paid my life of pain,
   One kiss immortal winged thee to thy rest!

IV.

Can I forget?—O, never, never more
    Thy virgin-widow's heart-pangs shall surcease;
Though till the agony of life pass o'er
    Grief cannot kill—or I had gone to peace.

V.

Still, " young and fair," men call me, and my ear
    Burns with the hot blood's tingling, when some sound,
Too like that voice the living may not hear,
    Renews the anguish of the bitter wound.

VI.

O memory of the yearning heart's desire,
    Sweet life of life outbreathed in mingling sighs,
Undying flame of love's soul-piercing fire,
    Shot by the lightning flash of wondrous eyes!

VII.

O time of love! for mortal mould too much
    The wealth of joy thy wild emotions bring;
How the soft pressure of his lightest touch
    Stirred in my veins the tumult of the spring!

VIII.

O death, what is in thee that **I should** fear?
   Thy bitterness is passed—thy sting forgot;
Hath thy dark **realm a** prison-house **more drear,**
   More cold than this dull world where **love is not?**

IX.

I know that " he shall **not** return **to me,**
   But I shall go to him"—O, my lost **love!**
Could I believe the All Merciful's decree
   But parted here to make **us one above¹**

X.

Farewell, farewell! though vanished, ever dear;
   Farewell, my only love! remember **me,**
Where'er with God **thou bidest, far** or near,
   Till He, our God, shall gather me to thee!

NOTES.

————o————

1. Captain Burke.
2. Iphigenia.
3. Marshall St. **Arnaud.**
4. Lord Raglan died June 28th, 1855.
5. The Emperor Nicholas died March, **1855.**
6. The **Salient of** the Redan was held **by our men for one hour and fifty six minutes**—Vide Russell, vol. **1, pp. 158, 159.**
7. Princess Carola Vasa.
8. Mayne's statue of **the Reading Girl.**
9. Pyrrhus.
10. The Abbey of Haute Combe.
11. Marino Faliero, Doge **of Venice, beheaded April 19th, 1355.**
12. Conradino, beheaded at Naples, **October 25th, 1268.**
13. Princess Charlotte Augusta of **Wales.**
14. A common superstition **at** Rome.
15. Miramar.
16. Hon. Augustus Winn.
17. Princess Salm Salm.
18. Queen Louise of **Prussia, mother of the Emperor William.**
19. Di voi, Pastor, s'accorse **il** Vangelista,
    Quando colei, che siede sovra l'acque,
    Puttaneggiar co'regi **a** lui fu vista :
 Quella che con le sette teste nacque,
    E dalle diece corna ebbe argomento,
    Fin che virtute al suo marito piacque.
 Fatto v'avete Dio d'oro e el'argento :
    E che altro è da voi al idolatre,
    Se non ch'egli uno, e voi n'orate **ceuto** ?
 Ahi, Costantin, di quanto mal fue matre,
    Non la tua conversion, ma quella dote
    Che da te prese il primo ricco patre !

Dante Inferno, Canto 19.

20. **At** Canosa, Henry IV. Emperor of Germany, submitted himself to Pope Gregory VII, who had deposed him from the Imperial Crown, and absolved his subjects from their allegiance, A. D. 1077.
21. The Barkut, or Golden Eagle, used in the East to chase deer : the bird fixes his talons in the back of the flying prey, and tears out and devours his liver.
22. **General Trochu.**

www.ingramcontent.com/pod-product-compliance
Lightning Source LLC
Chambersburg PA
CBHW060246030726
47493CB00025B/2792